Who cares about
elderly people?

illustrated by **Pam Adams**

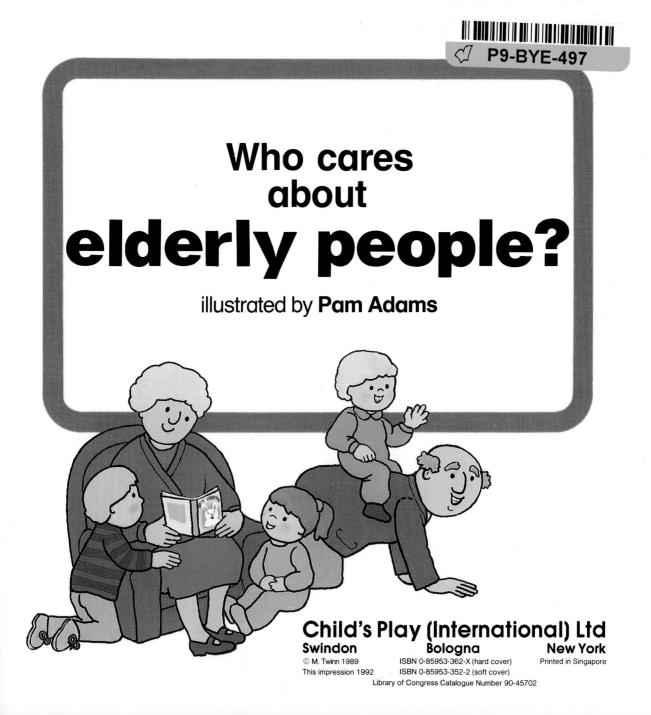

Child's Play (International) Ltd

Swindon   **Bologna**   **New York**

© M. Twinn 1989   ISBN 0-85953-362-X (hard cover)   Printed in Singapore

This impression 1992   ISBN 0-85953-352-2 (soft cover)

Library of Congress Catalogue Number 90-45702

Everybody grows old.
We all grow older all the time.

If you are three,
a twelve-year old brother
seems old.

If you are twelve,
your cousin seems old
at twenty-one.

Young people often wish they were older.
Old people always wish they were younger.

When you are old, you can't jump about
like you could when you were young.

Walking isn't always easy for old people.
Some have to use a stick.

Old people's eyes aren't as strong as they were,
and they probably need to wear glasses.

They may not hear well.
They may need a hearing aid.

They may need false teeth.

They can't always remember.
They may become absent-minded.

So, being old isn't all fun.
. . . But it isn't all bad, either.

You have more time to do what you want.
Like playing Golf . . .

. . . or painting pictures.

You may carry on working,
if you enjoy it.

As long as you are fit,
you might even run in a marathon.

**Young people
and old people
have a lot
to give each other.**

**Time spent
with old people
is never wasted.**

Old people may sit with us
when our parents have to go out.

It is fun, when they tell us about
when our parents were children,
or when they were young themselves.

When we are sad, they cheer us up.

And they have patience to mend things.

They enjoy teaching us to swim.

They will help us with our lessons.

They always have time to play games or tell a story.
They like it when we spend time with them.

But we must remember not to be noisy and to behave.
Otherwise, they get cross, just like our parents.

Some old people need help.
There are lots of things young people can do.

You can go shopping.

You can clean and tidy up.

You can make them a drink.

Or you can just talk and listen.

Old people sometimes look strange . . .
Especially if they have nobody to take care of them.

That's when you can be really helpful.

When you are friends, you don't notice age.